Unfamiliar Fruit
Volume I

Three out-of-the-ordinary stories by

BILL GOURGEY

Unfamiliar Fruit
Volume I

Jacked Arts
Washington, DC 20008
www.jackedarts.com

Library of Congress Control Number: 2012919390

ISBN-13:   978-0-9797435-4-2
ISBN-10:   0-9797435-4-0

For my friend Tim Petty

Such a long, long time to be gone
And a short time to be there

- The Grateful Dead, Box of Rain

Contents

Origami

By the time Sammy opened his eyes, the pelting rain had settled into a steady rhythm against his bedroom window. In the dim light, he felt himself drifting, caught in the disorienting current of his dreams. Was it morning or night? Weekend or school day? And why did he feel trapped in his bed?

As soon as he remembered what had awoken him, Sammy sat up in a panic and stared wildly around his basement room. Where was Dad? He tried to leap out of bed, but the sheets twisted and grabbed his legs like linen vines. Beads of sweat dotted his forehead and upper lip as he wrestled and kicked his way out, landing on the floor with a thud. Outside, the rain continued to thrum, playing its solemn tune.

Dad! Where are you? Before he had a chance to search further, Sammy's dream came back to him in a vivid, horrifying torrent. He had been playing outside with Dad when it started to rain. Hard. At first it was fun. Puddles formed quickly and spilled into brooks that rushed down the curb and cascaded through grates, echoing in the cavernous sewer. Sammy splashed and sloshed, laughing at the watery park that gushed through his dry, cinder-block neighborhood. He held Dad close to keep him from getting too wet.

But when Sammy tried to leap over a swimming pool of a puddle in his school's chain-linked playground the fun went bad. Lightning struck nearby, which startled Sammy and caused him to fall, mid-leap, into the pool-puddle. To save himself from drowning in the rising water, he let go of Dad. He watched helplessly as Dad swirled downstream toward an enormous iron grate that led into a dark, stony castle. Sammy tried to swim after Dad, but since he only knew how to doggy paddle it took forever, especially since his legs were bound together and hardly worked. By the time he reached the metal bars the water had subsided, and Dad, now soggy and translucent, drooped through the interstices. As Sammy tried to peel Dad free, he tore an arm, then the other, then Dad's legs, and finally his head. Sammy stared at the pasty pulp balled up in his hand and began to cry. The harder he cried, the harder it rained. He curled his fingers around Dad, squeezed the pieces into a ball, and shook his fist at the sad, angry sky.

Now that he was fully awake, Sammy shivered as he tried to free himself from the lingering shreds of nightmare. He reached for the light on his milk-crate nightstand and squinted as he tore through the books piled randomly on the floor beside his bed. Which book had he been reading last? He scratched his head, and his lip quivered. A tear welled. As he bent his head to wipe his nose with his wrist, his eyes fell on *The Rotten Island*, which had slid under his bed from its usual post at the top of the pile. Smiling with relief, he snatched the book from its hiding place and carefully opened the covers. There, holding his place at Sammy's favorite part of the story (where the first flower appears amidst the desolation, causing one of the monsters to lose his mind), there was Dad.

He caressed his precious, crumbling artifact; then he lifted it onto his bed. He ran his fingers along the ragged, grimy edges of Dad's head and arms. He vowed to add more tape to where Dad's torn foot flapped. He stroked Dad's pencil-dot nose and ran his finger along the straight line that formed his stoic mouth. Then he ruffled the creased flaps of hair that stood straight up from Dad's square head. Sammy didn't see the boxy, transformer features of his homemade doll because Dad had every loving paternal trait Sammy could think of. He didn't see the tears and tatters, the creases and crinkles, the spots and stains. Dad was perfect!

"Sammy! Time to get up," his mom called through the door, knocking lightly.

Instinctively, Sammy pulled his pillow over Dad to hide him. *Must be a school day*, Sammy thought. "OK, Mom!"

As his mother's steps retreated, Sammy returned to caressing Dad, allowing his awakening panic to recede. In its place, a blissful feeling grew. Sammy kept his eye on Dad while he dressed, not even realizing that his shirt was inside out and his shoes were on the wrong feet.

* * *

"I just want to remind you," Sammy's mother said, washing dishes while Sammy slouched at their small kitchen table, staring grumpily at his breakfast. "I will be home a little later than usual. I have to meet someone after school." Sammy's mom worked as a guidance counselor (whatever that was) at the high school, which had nearly the same schedule as Sammy's lower school.

"I remember," Sammy said flatly. He lifted his fork and pushed the eggs into cloud formations.

"Do you have the keys in your backpack?"

"I always do, Mom," Sammy said, sounding more irritated than he meant. His mother turned swiftly.

"Don't get cranky with—Oh, come on, Sammy," his mother said, abandoning one thought for another.

Sammy hated it when his mom didn't finish sentences.

"It took time to make that breakfast. I want you to eat that now, mister."

"OK, Mom," Sammy grumbled, slipping a good-faith morsel of egg into his mouth. His mother returned to her dishes.

"I was thinking," his mom said after a few minutes, during which Sammy flattened the eggs to make it look like he had eaten some, and nibbled the soft parts of his toast. "We should visit Aunt Barbara this weekend. She's invited us to sleep over."

"Do we have to?"

"You used to like Lincoln Park. We could go to the beach. It's probably still warm enough to swim in the lake."

"I just don't feel like it," Sammy muttered. And he didn't. His Aunt Barbara was nice and all, and so was his cousin, Morgan, who was two years older than Sammy, but visiting familiar places hurt—not like a scraped knee, more like a broken bone, like the time Sammy fractured his elbow when he fell off his bike. Everything looked OK, but it hurt even when he was lying still, even after they put the cast on. His dad had said it was because the damage was inside, under his skin. His dad.

"Well, I already told Aunt Barbara yes," Sammy's mom declared. "It will be good for both of us." After failing to balance the pan on the dish rack, she grabbed the dishtowel and turned to face Sammy while she dried it. She studied her listless son and frowned, shaking her head. She returned the pan to its cupboard.

"If you're not going to eat any eggs," his mother conceded, drying her hands on her apron, "at least eat your fruit."

Sammy wondered what kind of unfamiliar fruit his mother was serving him today. She'd been on a kick lately, as if changing what they ate would change their circumstances. "It's kiwi," his mother said, seeming to read his thoughts. "You used to love kiwi when you were younger."

When I was younger. The words clattered against Sammy's skull like the clapper of a bell. When he was younger he used to have breakfast with his dad who made a game of tasting even the weirdest looking stuff. When he was younger he used to stand in the bathroom singing pirate songs with his dad while he shaved: "Yoho, yoho," Sammy mouthed. *When I was younger—everything wasn't as serious as it is now, with you Mom!* He stared accusingly at his mom, who was hanging her apron distractedly, fumbling for the hook on the back of the door with one hand while scribbling something on the kitchen whiteboard, where she kept a running list of groceries and things she didn't want to forget. *She probably has a million things on her mind*, Sammy thought, *every one of them somewhere else than here—with me.*

4

As soon as his mom left the kitchen to finish getting ready, Sammy reached into his backpack and slipped Dad into his lap. "Yoho, yoho," he whispered, running his fingers in an o-ring around Dad's penciled mouth.

"What are you doing, Sammy?" his mother said, looking over his shoulder. Startled, Sammy jerked sideways, exposing Dad.

"Oh no, mister!" his mother snapped, grabbing Dad from his lap before Sammy could react. She crumpled his doll into a ball and shook her fist in the air. "I am sick and tired of seeing you carry this filthy scrap around," she said, her voice rising to an unbridled yell. "How many times have I told you to get rid of this—this trash?" Her knuckles turned white, reflecting the fury in her face. She hurled the ball into their garbage pail. "And this time I want it to stay there or so help me God!"

Despite his best effort, a tear escaped and slid down Sammy's cheek. His lip quivered, hastening the advance of the unwelcome display. He wiped the tear away with his wrist. Sammy hated his mom. Hated her more than anything in the world. Hated her mostly because she was not his dad.

His mom slid into the seat beside him. "Oh Sammy," she said, propping her elbows on the table and burying her face in her hands. His mom was like that—one moment angry, the next sad—as ominous and unpredictable as a summer storm. His dad was never like that.

"Oh, Sammy," she said again, laying her hand on the table, gesturing for her son to take it. "You have to let him go—"

"He's coming back, Mom!" Sammy snapped, folding his arms and leaning back.

"No, Son, he's not."

"How do you know?"

"I just know. It's time to clean out the skeletons from our closet. Time to let him go."

What skeletons? Sammy wondered. Was his dad dead? His mom had never mentioned that before. "Well, you're wrong! You're wrong about everything! Dad's watching out for us. I know he is. He'll be back. You'll see!"

5

"Oh Sammy," his mother whispered, leaning over to touch his shoulder. Sammy jerked away. "Fine," his mother said, recoiling angrily from her son's rejection. "But let's get something straight. Your father left, not me. So don't take it out on me. And when I tell you he's not coming back, he's not. Period. God is the only one watching out for us. He's the only compassionate one around here. So if you're looking for a savior, I suggest you turn to someone more reliable." His mother pressed her hair with her palms to straighten it. She stood, looking down at Sammy with equal parts pity and scorn. "I don't want to see that piece of trash around here ever again," she said, pointing to the garbage. "Or you'll be in big trouble." She turned and walked swiftly down the hall, calling to him. "You better be ready in five! And finish that fruit!"

God, shmod, Sammy thought, nibbling on a piece of kiwi and spitting it onto his plate to spite his mom. What good had God done his mom? For all her praying and church, she was the unhappiest person he knew. No. If Sammy had to put his faith anywhere, it would be in his dad—a flesh-and-blood being who would someday come again. He carried his plate over to the garbage can and carefully scraped away the food, taking care not to cover or sully Dad. Standing there, staring into the scraps, a plan formed. He would have to save Dad before his dad could save him. *He* would be *Dad's* savior.

* * *

The first thing Sammy did when he opened the front door was to call out, "Mom, I'm home." He had to be sure that the coast was clear. He called again, and when no one answered, he threw down his backpack and ran to the kitchen. He opened the lid to the garbage and smiled. There was Dad. A piece of kiwi had slid on top, and his mom must have emptied something wet into the trash because Dad felt as soggy as a giant spitball, but Sammy knew he could revive him. He placed the lump of Dad on the linoleum floor and ran to the bathroom. A few minutes later, he had his mom's hair dryer plugged into the outlet she used for the beater. He began to peel apart the crumpled ball, drying it a little, then teasing out a crease, then drying it some more. He made a few more trips to the bathroom, returning with tweezers, band aids, and hairspray, which his mom used to stiffen her hair.

Sammy knew he had a little more than an hour before his mom came home. He worked quickly, but cautiously, with the care and focus of a surgeon.

As he often did, Sammy thought about the time he had made the paper doll—with his real dad. Sammy had come running into the living room holding a pair of scissors high, thrusting them into the air like a sword, exultant that he had control of a grown-up's tool.

"Whoa there, buddy!" his dad had said, laughing as he snatched the scissors away. "You can't run around like that." Sammy felt the sting of his dad's casual rebuke. His dad seemed to see it. "You know how to use these things?"

Sammy shook his head and pouted.

"Well, all right. First things first. You gotta learn how to carry them before you learn how to cut with them." His dad showed him how to cover up the point with his fist. Sammy carried the scissors to the kitchen. They sat at the table cutting and folding shapes from scraps of paper.

Sammy remembered his dad's smell more than he remembered anything. Spicy but minty. Like the aftershave that sat in the bathroom drawer for a long time until his mom finally got rid of it. And another smell, a damp one, like his dad was always sweating or something.

Sammy remembered piecing some of the scraps together. "Look at that, little man," his dad said, smiling as he leaned over Sammy's work. "That's origami."

Origami. The word had sounded like a magic spell that could bring his paper creation to life.

"Let me get some tape," his dad had said. Then he helped Sammy tape the pieces together. "What you gonna name him?"

Sammy thought for a moment. "Dad."

His dad ruffled his hair and said, "Well, then, we better give him some hair." That's when his dad showed him how to cut little incisions in a row. Sammy ruffled the paper with the same loving effect.

Dad was more than two years old now. Sammy stared at the pulpy figure, crumpled and creased so many times that the paper felt as soft and worn as his old blanket. Momentarily setting aside the hair dryer, Sammy applied some hairspray and a band aid to the back of Dad's neck. Satisfied, he resumed drying the doll.

As the dryer whined, he thought about the day his dad didn't come home. Sammy had been waiting on the magazine rack, by the front door, as he always did when the little hand touched the five. By the time it had reached the six, he heard his mother shouting and crying in the kitchen. As it got close to the seven, his mother came into the room and sat on the edge of the couch, a wad of tissues crumpled in her hands. Her eyes were red, and her nose was too.

"Let's get you some dinner," she'd said to Sammy in a hoarse whisper.

"I'm waiting for Dad," Sammy said, knowing something was wrong, but convinced that remaining at his usual post would be the best way to fix it.

"Dad's not coming home tonight," his mother said softly.

"But why not?" Sammy asked, his bottom lip jutting out like a pink eraser.

"Because," his mother said, pulling at the tissue and wiping her eyes. "He's—he's busy."

She had used the same excuse for a week when Sammy finally refused to leave the magazine rack. "Where's Dad?" he demanded, lips trembling with fear and fury.

"He's not coming home," his mother said. "He's never coming home, Sammy." She reached for Sammy's hands. "I'm sorry. So, so sorry." Sammy didn't believe her. He ran to his room and slammed the door.

When Aunt Barbara and Morgan came to stay with them for a few weeks, Sammy knew his mom was right.

"Why?" he kept asking.

"I don't know," his mother replied.

Sammy kept the hair dryer focused on Dad like a ray of hot sun.

After a month of missing his dad, Sammy became convinced that he'd done something wrong. He kept telling his mom that he promised to be really good if his dad came home again. "It's not about you, honey," she assured him. But it *was* about him, wasn't it? If his dad really loved him, he would never leave him. No matter what his mother said, she could never explain away that simple fact. She called his dad selfish, said he had fallen in love with someone else, and said he was irresponsible. But Sammy knew that somehow he had been a disappointing son.

Dad's frayed edges seemed the most susceptible. The paper tendrils began to curl under the intense heat. Thin, hardly perceptible threads of smoke spiraled away. The tips of Dad's white hair turned brown. Sammy seemed not to notice as he kept the dryer trained on the fragile puppet.

He thought he had seen his dad once. At the grocery store. But it couldn't have been his dad because the man abruptly turned around and disappeared around the head of the aisle. But it must have been his dad because his mom cursed and swore all the way home and made Sammy go to bed early.

Sammy thought about that. And he thought about all the things his mom had said about his dad. *It's not about you, honey.* The words flitted and darted in his head like neon fish. It *was* about him. After all, his dad was *his dad.* No one else was his dad. But maybe his mom was right about one thing. Maybe his dad *was* selfish. After all, he left without saying good-bye. Without leaving a note. Without coming back to say Happy Birthday or Merry Christmas. His dad had missed Sammy's race-car costume, the one he and his mom had built from a box for Halloween. And he missed Sammy losing his first tooth. He had lost several since then. His dad missed everything. Sammy's concentrated expression transformed as he considered how his dad had stopped caring. Worse, he had stopped loving him—and his mom. How could that be? What had they done wrong? He couldn't think of anything so bad that it would have caused his dad to cut them off—like paper limbs.

The fruity fragrance of his mom's hairspray suddenly turned acrid. Sammy smelled smoke. The unbandaged edges of his doll had turned brown and begun to curl. Suddenly, Dad's hair burst into flame. Sammy fell back, yanking the hair dryer's plug from the wall, causing a giant spark that arced across the kitchen counter. Sammy retreated like a crab to the corner of the kitchen, watching in horror as Dad flashed into an inferno, then quickly petered out. He thought about dousing the smoldering ashes with water, but then Sammy had another idea.

He remained rooted in the corner, watching as Dad shrank to a pile of gray and white ash sitting delicately atop the sticky remains of tape and band aid. When Sammy felt it was safe, he rummaged under the sink where his mom kept glass jars to store hot grease. With great care, he swept Dad's remains into an old pickle jar and screwed the top on. He set Dad aside while he cleaned the linoleum with paper towels and a sponge. Sammy finished the job, returning the hair dryer and other operating tools to the bathroom. Finally, he took the jar into the living room and set it on the mantle above their faux fireplace. He made room next to the colorful ceramic urn containing the ashes of his grandfather—his mom's dad.

* * *

"Hi, Sammy!" his mom called. Sammy was sitting in the kitchen with his composition book and pencil. "Hi, Mom," he called back with a clear and steady voice. His mom walked into the kitchen and kissed his forehead.

"Were you making toast?" she asked, sniffing the air.

"Yep," Sammy replied, smiling.

His mom smiled back, happy to see her son expressing something other than a frown. "Looks like you had a good day," she said, unloading items from her grocery bag.

Sammy nodded.

"What were you doing?" his mom asked.

"Cleaning out my closet," Sammy said matter-of-factly, but his grin gave away the measure of his good mood.

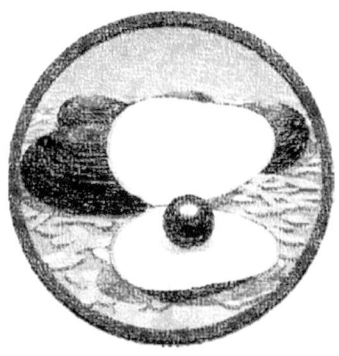

Millennium Pearl

"Hey, Mom," Laura said, charging into the tiny office, separated from the shop's retail space by a red velvet curtain salvaged from First Trinity's latest rummage sale.

"Oh dear, don't do that!" Michelle said, pressing her hand to her chest to steady her thudding heart. "You startled me."

"I always do," Laura grinned. She grabbed her mother's hand. "Come on. There's someone I want you to meet."

"Just a minute, darling," Michelle said. "You know I'm not very good with numbers, and I really must finish these last few entries, or I'll have to start all over again." Michelle returned to transcribing numbers into the ledger.

"I'll get 'em for you later," Laura told her. "Promise." She crossed herself and grinned again, stretching out the metal rings that lined her upper lip like an armored caterpillar.

Her mother smiled. "Well, that's thoughtful," she said, knowing that Laura could not be trusted to honor her oath. It had been a long time since she could count on Laura for any help at all.

"Who am I meeting?" Michelle asked, pressing her syrup-brown dress flat to remove wrinkles that weren't there. She slipped her feet back into the cream crepe-sole shoes tucked neatly to the side of her chair.

"It's a surprise."

"I don't like surprises."

"You'll like this one," Laura insisted. "I do!" She looked side-long at her mother.

"At least give me a hint," Michelle said, laughing nervously. "Animal, mineral—"

"Animal." Laura folded her arms and tapped her steel-tipped boots, anticipating her mother's response, whose body language predictably asked for another clue. "Male."

"Well, then, give me a moment to do something with this hair." Michelle's hair hung to her loins like a drape. Cut as meticulously across the back as her ramrod bangs in front, there wasn't much for her to do other than spin it up into an oversized bun, which she did.

The effort seemed comical to her daughter, whose own purple coif was too short to do anything with but mousse into thorny rows.

When Michelle stalled some more by reaching for the clear lip gloss, Laura grabbed her mother's arm. "Come on already, Mom. It's not a Texas beauty pageant."

Laura dragged her mother past the curtain. A young man dressed in the same black leather and steel-ring jerkin as Laura leaned nonchalantly on one of the showcases. He flicked a heavy key ring, tethered to his drooping pants, and adjusted its orbit every time he twisted his wrist so that the spirals widened. Concentrating on his game, the idle young man worked a wad of tobacco tucked into his lower lip.

"Gray, this is Michelle," Laura said, punching him playfully on the shoulder. "Mom, meet Gray."

"How do you do, Gray?" Michelle stretched out her arm as straight as a winch.

"Ma'am," Gray said, standing up suddenly and dropping the keys to grasp her hand in a limp shake. The keys swung back into the glass case, threatening to crack it. "Sorry 'bout that," he mut-tered, hitching the ring to his belt.

14

"Gray's my boyfriend," Laura announced as easily as she would a change in the weather.

Michelle froze. Time stretched like a rubber band as Laura stared at her mom, Michelle stared at Gray, and Gray stared at his feet. Annoyed by her mom's cold scrutiny, Laura snapped the awkward moment of silence. "I keep telling Gray about your shop and all, so we just thought we would stop by."

"That's very thoughtful. How old are you, Gray?" Michelle asked.

"Mom, don't start with the thousand questions," Laura moaned. She stepped in beside Gray to square off with her mother.

"It's hardly—"

"Eighteen, ma'am," Gray muttered, attempting to meet Michelle's intractable gaze.

"You are aware that Laura is only sixteen—"

"What the hell does that have to do with anything?" Laura demanded, grabbing Gray's hand. "Besides, I'll be seventeen in a few weeks."

"I was just pointing out—"

"You weren't 'just' doing anything, Mom."

"It's OK, babe," Gray said, squeezing Laura's hand.

"No, it's not OK," Laura said, turning on Gray. "I knew—"

"Knew what, dear?" It was Michelle's turn to get defensive. "That I would want to know—"

"That you would be a cold-hearted bitch if I brought Gray over to meet you," Laura told her mother, jutting out her chin as if daring her to strike.

"Babe," Gray said quietly, trying to reign in Laura's outburst.

"I will not listen to that kind of language," Michelle snapped. "I expect—"

"You expect too much," Laura said, shaking her head. "Let's go, Gray, we're outta here."

"Where are you going?" Michelle asked.

"What does it matter? As long as I'm away from here," Laura said, stomping toward the door.

"Nice to meet you, ma'am," Gray said, turning to look Michelle in the eye for the first time.

When the door slammed shut, the string of bells tied to the door's frame rattled angrily and a small oyster-shell brooch with a black pearl set in its center fell off a nearby counter. The shell withstood the fall, but the pearl popped off and rolled under a stool.

Michelle stood transfixed. The broken brooch and its liberated pearl registered, but she seemed unable to respond. Her cluttered shop—crammed full of knickknacks, small antiques, old books, and almost every manner of gratuitous collectible—closed in on her. Her chest constricted, and she struggled for air. She felt lightheaded. She staggered forward, leaned heavily on the stool that loomed protectively over the dark pearl, and gasped. It took longer than usual to recover. Michelle's anxiety attacks had continued to lengthen and intensify. She knew she should see a doctor, but she feared the prognosis. Worse, she abhorred the idea of medicating away her problems.

A few minutes later, the bells jingled. A customer stepped into the store, providing Michelle the impetus to deflect the wave of anxiety. "Welcome," she said, "to Turn."

"I was driving by," said the customer, a fleshy woman dressed in pastel patterns and smelling cloy, like dying flowers. "And I saw your shop's name—Turn, Turn, Turn—and I thought how clever. Ecclesiastes. So I turned," she said and laughed.

Michelle smiled. It pleased her whenever a customer identified with her shop's name; she usually offered them a deep discount.

* * *

Later that night, when Laura rolled in the door to their apartment above the shop, Michelle put down her book and slipped out of bed. She rarely waited up for Laura anymore, but tonight she couldn't sleep.

"I can hear you, Mom. What are you doing up?" Laura said, peering over the refrigerator door.

Michelle stepped into the kitchen, wearing her threadbare, baby blue nightgown with yellowed ruffles framing the neckline, and matching silk dance slippers. Her hair hung in its place.

"Your eyes are red," Michelle said.

"So?"

"And you smell like booze."

"You figured that out on your own?" Laura said, leaning heavily on the refrigerator door.

"I don't appreciate that kind of sass."

"And I don't appreciate being treated like a tween." Laura returned to rummaging through the fridge.

"Snacking like that isn't going to help you lose some of that weight you've been gaining," Michelle said, regretting instantly the comment. She wanted to have a conversation with Laura, find out more about her boyfriend, and apologize for their fight in the shop, which wouldn't happen if she didn't stop criticizing. "Why don't you join me at the gym sometime?" she offered, hoping to recover, but only managing to make things worse. Michelle's dedication to the gym—to maintaining a trim, tight physique that spoke of discipline with no hint of indulgence—was second only to her devotion to her church.

"I'll get as fat as I want," Laura said. She slammed the refrigerator door, dumped an armful of Tupperwared leftovers on the counter, and pulled up her shirt to show off her belly. She slapped her gut and pinched a roll of fat on her hips. "Takes a lot of food to eat for two."

"What's that supposed to mean?" Michelle asked, refusing to make the obvious connection.

"That I'm pregnant, Mom," Laura said with indifference as she opened a Tupperware lid to sample its contents.

"What?" Michelle gasped.

"You heard me." Chewing on a chicken leg, Laura turned and stared at her mother.

"How do you know?" Michelle whispered as if daring to speak normally would expose her daughter's taboo. She pressed her hand to her lips to keep any more undesirable contents from spilling out.

"Do you wanna see the strip?" Laura asked, reaching for another container. "Isn't there anything sweet in this house?"

"But how?"

"You should know," Laura said and laughed. "You had me. And I know that was no immaculate conception." She laughed again, more cynically this time.

"Please," Michelle pleaded. She slid into one of the four matching folding chairs that surrounded their small, round table. A stencil on the back of the chair read, "First Trinity."

"I mean who, when?"

"Well, you met him today. And by the way, that went well," Laura scoffed, chewing a mouthful of dry potato salad. "And the doctor at Planned Parenthood says seven weeks."

"At least there's still time for—Planned Parenthood?"

"Well, I wasn't exactly going to go see Dr. Oliver," Laura said, referring to her lifelong pediatrician. "Still time for what?" Laura narrowed her eyes at her mother.

"Oh, Laura!" Michelle sobbed, burying her face in her hands.

"Just what I expected," Laura said, shaking her head.

"What else did you expect?" Michelle asked, wiping tears from her cheeks with her bare hands.

"How about congratulations? You're gonna be a grandma, after all."

"Congratulations?" Michelle could feel the initial wave of shock give way to frustration. Her face flushed. "My God, Laura, you're only sixteen—"

"Seventeen."

"You're still in high school!"

"You were just out of high school when you had me."

"I don't want you repeating my mistakes," Michelle blurted.

"So now I'm a mistake," Laura said. "Fuck you too, Mom."

"That's not what I meant."

"But it's what you said. Or do you always say things you don't mean?" Laura knew she could always outdebate her mother, who flustered easily.

"This is not some game, young lady, and it's not just *your* life, anymore."

"Well, that's great advice coming from someone who only thinks about herself," Laura quipped. She reached for another container and unbuttoned her pants to liberate her belly. Laura wasn't fat, not by a long stretch, but she had allowed soft curves to form around her lanky frame—mostly to differentiate her physique from her mom's.

"I won't have that kind of—"

"I won't have this, I won't have that," Laura mimicked. "You sound like a scratched disc."

"You ungrateful little," Michelle screeched.

"Bitch! I'll finish the sentence for you, Mom."

"After all I've done for you and without any help from any-one."

"And why is that, Mom?" Laura asked. She pulled out a chair and swung it around to straddle it. "I'll answer that. You chased off Dad. Gram and Gramps can't stand you. You never go out. Your life revolves around the shop downstairs, church, and the gym. Face it, Mom, you don't have any friends. You've even succeeded in chasing me off." Laura sat back and rubbed her exposed belly. She wasn't sure why she felt so calm, tearing down her mother's world. She felt no remorse even as she watched her mother suc-cumb to another panic attack. "I'll get you a glass of water," she offered.

"Don't—you—do—a—thing," Michelle choked. She took sev-eral deep breaths and pressed her palms flat on the table for sup-port. "How dare you criticize me. I've given you a good life. I've built a profitable business. I have friends at the gym, friends at church. If I don't go out much it's because I'm too exhausted mak-ing a living to…" She snapped her mouth shut before something else fell out that she might regret.

"Have it your way, Mom," Laura said, still amazed by how calm she continued to remain. "But I wouldn't call those people at the gym or church your friends. When's the last time you went out with them, invited them to dinner, or sat down and had a heart-to-heart? Just because you see them every day or every week doesn't make them your friends. They're just as fucked up as you are, looking for escapes from their disappointing lives. When's the last time you confided in anyone but your precious God? You're alone, Mom, face it."

In the interest of self-preservation, Michelle tuned Laura out. She closed her eyes to listen to the voice of Karen, who ran Tuesday's yoga hour at the gym. "Breath in, breath out. Feel each breath touch your core." In. Out.

When Michelle opened her eyes, she felt calmer, even though her hands still trembled. "If you don't like my life," she said quietly, "then don't follow in my footsteps."

"I'm not," Laura said, reaching over to the counter for the nearest unopened container.

"Getting pregnant so young, marrying your high school sweetheart—"

"Marry?" Laura wrinkled her nose at the dry tuna salad lurking beneath the lid. "Who said anything about marrying Gray? He's cool and everything, but I don't plan on spending the rest of my life with him."

"But your child?"

"You raised me on your own."

"But—"

"But what?" Laura sneered. "Aren't you happy with the outcome?"

"Of course—"

"LIAR!" Laura screamed. Like plate glass struck by a wayward stone, her calm façade shattered. She threw the container against the wall. Tuna splattered and stuck like wet sawdust. "You can't stand me, and you know it. You think I'm some kind of freak. Well, that's what I think you are, Mom. A freak!"

"I won't have this." Michelle stood and stepped away from the table.

"Fuck you, Mom!" Laura stood too, and she stepped in close to her mother, daring her to strike first, aching for physical confrontation, something to snap the tension that had been building for years.

Michelle stepped back and dropped to her knees. She clasped her hands together and bowed her head, rocking back and forth as she prayed.

Laura shoved her mother's shoulders. "You have something to say?" she shouted. "Say it to me. To my face. I'm here, not there."

Laura pointed to the ceiling, the roof beyond, and the sky beyond that, which terminated somewhere in the heavens. "I'm outta here. You're on your own now, Mom. You have no one left but God. It's what you've always wanted. Don't try to find me."

Moments later the door slammed with such force that, for the second time that day, something slid off a counter—none other than the oyster brooch, which Michelle had brought upstairs from the shop to repair. This time, the lustrous black pearl clacked as it bounced across the linoleum kitchen floor until it settled under the table.

* * *

Michelle could not sleep. After Laura left, she had taken a shower. Try as she might, however, she could not scrub away the grit agitating her soul. Although she had repeated the motions that defined her bedtime routine, sleep eluded her. How could it not? Laura's words echoed over and over.

Not too long ago, Michelle had heard a poem presented by one of her church members in their weekly reading group. She didn't like poetry, didn't like having to work for the hidden meaning. But when he presented Robert Frost's poem, *Bereft*, as a celebration of the Almighty, Michelle did not have to work at it to see that the presenter had missed the point. The poem frightened her, but it also drew her in. She saw uncanny parallels between her own life and that of the poem's narrator. She made a copy and brought it home. One night she mustered the courage to read it. Then she read it again. And so on until it finally earned a place beside her alarm clock. Now, the poem's voice spoke unbeckoned; its words coiled around her solitude:

Word I was in the house alone somehow must have gotten abroad,
word I was in my life alone, word I had no one left but God.

She had chosen not to argue the point at the reading group that such a barren image could not be a celebration of anything, let

21

alone faith. And then Laura had hurled that very refrain at her, almost verbatim, and its fangs sank deep into her soul.

Michelle peeled back the covers and sat on the edge of her bed. Shivering, she rose and walked the few steps to her window, which overlooked the shop's parking lot and the two-lane highway beyond. Now and then a gust of wind rattled the window, sneaked through the cracks, and moaned. A car approached, slowed in front of her lot just enough for her anxious heart to skip a beat, but continued past, accelerating as it disappeared behind the swaying trees. Michelle slumped to the floor. The blinds sliced the street light into narrow bands that illuminated her face and trembling chest. She crossed herself and said three Hail Marys. After several moments of silent reflection, Michelle began to speak openly to her God, as if he had entered the room riding in on the wind and the striated rays of fluorescent light.

"Please, Lord, help me to help my Laura," she said in a tone more demanding than she intended. "I know she has not been faithful, but if *my* faith means anything to you, share with me now your divine wisdom." Michelle bowed her head, squeezed her eyes, and rocked back and forth, hands clasped like vises. The wind took up the poet's urgent refrain: *My secret must be known.*

Michelle's faith did not allow her to contemplate sources, only aspects; so when she heard a response in clear and distinct language, she nearly fell over with fright without questioning its origin or authenticity.

"Let her be," the voice said. For an instant, the streetlight flared, and the wind paused. Michelle nodded vigorously as if she agreed, but she did not. With her head still bowed to the two-toned light, she opened one eye and peered around the room.

"But how can I let her be when she doesn't even know what to be?" Michelle asked as humbly as she could, trying too obviously to strike a note of humility, but squeaking instead like a mouse.

"Who does?" the voice said. The wind resumed, gusting until the window rattled. Michelle's eyebrows nearly crashed into each other trying to make sense of such hallowed words. This seemed like the arcane and aggravating advice of her mother—or ex.

"Of course," she agreed. "But we at least know what she shouldn't be. Don't we?" At the last second Michelle tried to turn her defensive statement into a question, but she achieved mostly another squeak.

"Who's 'we'?" the voice said, sounding a little too tongue and cheek to reconcile with Michelle's expectations of almightiness.

"Well, I mean, I know she's not ready to be a mother. Especially a single mother."

"Were you?"

"Well, no. But I was more resourceful than she is."

"How do you know?"

Some things Michelle didn't need to know, to know. Frustrated, Michelle sloughed off decorum as naturally and subconsciously as if it were a constricting skin. "I'm her mother for God's sake!" She clapped her hand to her mouth, and her eyes grew wide.

But the voice did not seem to take offense. "What's her favorite beer?" it asked.

"She's not supposed to drink."

"How many tattoos does she have?"

"Those hideous things?"

"What does she do every day after school?"

"She used to help me at the shop."

"I rest my case."

"What does any of this have to do with Laura's—her predicament?"

"You said she wasn't resourceful enough."

"And?"

"You hardly know even the most superficial things about your daughter."

Who was this impostor in the room? A being as wise and full of love and forgiveness as her Lord would not stoop to such picayune banter. Tattoos and beer! Hah! And yet. He had a point. How well *did* Michelle know her daughter? When she was younger, maybe. When Laura loved and believed in whatever Michelle loved and believed in. That had been a long time ago. Years. In fact, for longer than she could admit Michelle and Laura had been on ever more divergent tracks. Desolation filled the distance between.

Michelle could not recall the last time she had spoken earnestly with her daughter without fighting. When was the last time she had paid Laura a heartfelt compliment? Why had she not seen them growing apart? It was as if a galaxy had yawned between them overnight. But it hadn't been overnight. She saw it all so clearly now. Had she been granted *His* view? Had *He* allowed her to step outside herself?

"Tell me, Lord," Michelle asked, feeling small. "What happens if you—diverge?"

"Diverge from what?" the voice asked.

Michelle thought for a moment. "Well—*For the grace of God hath appeared, bringing salvation to all men, instructing us, to the intent that, denying ungodliness and worldly lusts, we should live soberly and righteously and godly in this present world.*"

"I wouldn't worry about the tattoos," the voice said, reading Michelle's mind. "Some are quite striking. True acts of love."

Michelle's heart skipped a beat, and she missed a breath or two. Not only had she been caught allowing, as usual, trifles to obscure the true issues she should be confronting (how had *He* known she was thinking about Laura's tattoos and piercings, trying to count them from memory?), but also she could not believe that her God would admire the beauty of such defiling things. Perhaps this was a trap. After all, traps beset the faithful. But she had become adept at spotting even the subtlest. She sensed that she was being deliberately misled and provoked for almost suggesting to Laura earlier that she should abort her fetus. Michelle trembled. She had to know.

"Well, what about the sacredness of conception and the innocence of the unborn?" she asked fearfully.

"Isn't it hard enough worrying about the born?" the voice asked. "If your daughter decides to have her baby, be there for her. If she chooses not to, be there for her. Is that too much to ask?"

"But..." Michelle stammered, absorbing at once the odd sensations of cool relief and hot confusion.

"No buts. This one's simple. It is far more blessed to fight on behalf of those already in need. If you want to do something for the unborn, then preserve the beauty and abundance of the world they will inherit.

"For the record, what you started to suggest to your daughter tonight was the most courageous advice you've almost given her. I like courageous. It's what got this whole thing called creation started in the first place."

"But…" Michelle choked, unable to pluck a complete thought from the maelstrom in her mind. Or was the wind roaring in the room? She had lost focus. "But why do you speak to me in such—such a commonplace way? I—I thought—"

"If you prefer I could use click phonemes."

Michelle heard snaps and pops that sounded like the strange language of a tribe she'd seen on the History channel. Confused and scared, she covered her ears and hunkered down.

"I didn't think so," the voice said.

"But I expected something more—"

"More obscure?"

"Blessed," Michelle countered.

"No thanks. People have become too literal. It's time to keep the cards on the table."

"But—"

"No more buts. You want advice? Wisdom? Here it is, a once-in-a-millennium pearl: There is no evil. And there is no good. There is only knowledge. So relax. Get to know your daughter. Let her be. She will. And you might be pleasantly surprised."

The voice fell silent, but Michelle needed more, something to polarize the blinding luster of this gem born in the night among fluorescent stripes of light and a wind that wouldn't quit. Sensing her need, perhaps, the voice accommodated. "The absence of knowledge is folly. If you're looking for paths, stay off that one. It leads only to hate. And remember, actions speak louder than words."

As if the channeling of divine energy could only end in a short circuit, the streetlight winked out, leaving Michelle alone in the darkness of her bedroom. The wind died too. Seconds, minutes, hours passed, or maybe none at all. And still Michelle did not move, afraid, perhaps, that she might fall. When the earth quakes, it takes time to trust in it again.

* * *

Michelle awoke in the dark. She sat up in bed and realized she was naked. She must have fallen asleep after her shower. The streetlight across the parking lot filtered through the Venetian blinds just as she had imagined in her dream. Her dream! Michelle did not know where even to begin to digest such unfamiliar fruit. And yet she did not deny that she must. For the first time in her life she questioned not her faith so much as its source. An inner voice? A dead poet? A supernatural being? But even as she questioned it, she knew it didn't matter. Somehow, the sublime advice—the millennium pearl—agreed with her constitution even as it defied her protocol. It made sense. What was more, as unconventional as it might have been, there was no denying her prayer had been answered. She only hoped she still had the chance and good sense to follow it. One thing she knew after the brief vision: She did not want to be left alone with God, mostly because it was clear *He* did not want to be left with her. At that, a sorrowful smile sneaked across her face.

In the darkness, she reached for the phone on her nightstand and dialed a precious number by heart. When Laura answered, sobbing, Michelle knew she'd been saved—this time, by someone no less divine than her own daughter.

Amerigo's Foot

When Amerigo awoke to the smell of eggs and sausage, two familiar thoughts hit him at once: *Man, my stomach hurts!* and *¿Por qué siempre tengo tanta hambre?* By thirteen, Amerigo had watched the scale sail past three hundred pounds. Now, at sixteen, he'd added more than half of his thirteen-year-old self. Appetite dictated every waking moment of his day, even when he tried to think of the other things consuming most sixteen-year-old boys. His few friends called him an eating machine and would tease that the scent of a Wendy's French fry a mile off could distract him, even with the stench and fumes of twenty city blocks in between. At the Chelsea Ten Cinema, the crinkle of a candy wrapper three rows down would disrupt his focus as fully as if someone had shouted, "Fire!" Worse, like a heroin addict, his cravings would awaken him from deep sleep.

But this morning Amerigo felt surprisingly refreshed. He'd not had trouble breathing during the night; his heart, which had developed stress flutters last year, felt eerily regular, and he felt himself couched comfortably within the confines of his mattress—morning usually meant liberating some fold of his anatomy from painful pinching. Without preparing for the effort, which generally involved scooching to the edge of his bed where he would rock himself off and onto his knees, a process that took nearly five minutes, Amerigo sat up. Just like that. And two more thoughts hit him: *Dio mio! What the hell happened to the rest of me?* and *Could it be my prayers were answered?*

Thinking that he was still in a dream, Amerigo tried to leap out of bed, but when his foot hit the floor, he heard the wood planks crack under the carpet, and his bedroom shuddered with Richter-scale effect.

"Amerigo, qué pasa?" his mother called from the kitchen.

"Nada, Ma. I'm OK," Amerigo called back. And he was. For the first time since his days playing on monkey bars, Amerigo could see his navel, which had emerged from its clammy, blubbery hideout, and his penis hung grandly where it should, no longer reduced to spelunking its way through fleshy strata to perform its duties; he marveled at his shapely thighs, which had reappeared from beneath a gelatinous, abdominal canopy that usually stretched to his knees. He rotated his arms and raised them toward the ceiling—an effort that, just last night, would have ached and felt like lifting barbells.

A smile began to lift his now angular cheeks. "Un miracolo," he whispered, slipping into one of the three tongues spoken interchangeably at home—the one he reserved for his most impassioned moments. But even as the reality of the miracle sank in, so his gaze settled on the monstrosity replacing his right foot.

If Michelangelo had taken his chisel to stone with the fabled angles of Pablo Picasso, the result might have looked something like the gargoyle attached to Amerigo's Achilles heel. It was three times the size of his other foot, gray as stone, smooth as marble, but flexible enough to meet basic ambulatory specifications—that is, if it weren't so heavy.

On Amerigo's first attempt to walk toward his bedroom door (he couldn't wait to examine his svelte physique in the bathroom mirror) he nearly pulled a thigh muscle, and he fell over, landing with another thud.

"Amerigo!" his mother called.

"I'll be right down," Amerigo shouted in a panic. He wasn't yet ready to face others.

"Vámonos," his mother called. "You'll miss breakfast." Ordinarily, such a threat would have motivated Amerigo from even the most intense state of inertia, but at the moment all he could do was simultaneously marvel at his limber body and frown at his concrete foot.

On his second attempt, Amerigo was able to drag his leaden extremity across the floor, bunching the rug along the way. By the time he reached the half-inch threshold at his bedroom door, it looked as daunting as the Rocky Mountains to a traveler from the Great Plains. Still, with only minor bangs, Amerigo scaled the piedmont and dragged his foot into the bathroom across the hall.

He stared at the strange face in the mirror. Smiling, he worked his fingers carefully but steadily across his cheeks and chin. He studied his chest and his arms, flexing them to admire their definition. Muscles. Veins. Tendons. Bone. As far as he could tell, fat had been holding him together all of these years. Gobs of it. Not anymore. His smile broadened until his teeth showed. Even his gums had shrunk to allow his teeth to dictate his smile.

He turned to the full-length mirror behind the door and sucked in his stomach. He laughed. He could actually see a ripple of ribs emerge and project over the concavity of his retracted abdomen. He ran his hands across his belly and sides. His skin felt like velvet. Unexpected tears slid down his cheeks. He wiped them away with the backs of his wrists and sniffled. When his gaze reached his legs, however, he frowned. There stood his foot in all its gravestone glory. Amerigo bent to touch it. It tingled and seemed to pulse. He tried to lift his leg, but he could only achieve a slight shuffle. He wiggled the swollen, paw-like toes.

His mother called to him again. "I'm coming up," she hollered.

"Be right down, Mom!" Frantically, Amerigo grabbed a towel and wrapped it around his leg, hiding, barely, his superhero-sized extremity.

When he opened the bathroom door, his mother looked at him and shrieked. She turned and stumbled down the stairs, wailing to her husband, "Luigi, Luigi, un extraño, aquí, aquí!"

"No, Ma, it's me!" Amerigo shouted, shuffling after her. "It's Amerigo."

Amerigo's mother peered around the doorway and looked up at the stranger. She frowned. "You are not my son. What have you done with him?" But she stepped out farther for a closer look.

Amerigo smiled. "Mira! It is me, Ma." He turned slowly, straining to pull his foot without losing the towel.

"No lo sé," Amerigo's mother whispered, holding her hand to her mouth as she climbed the steps one at a time, scrutinizing the impostor who called himself her son. "Where is the rest of you?" she asked, dry-mouthed, voice cracking. "It does look like my boy," she admitted as she reached the step below Amerigo. "And it sounds like him." She poked Amerigo in the ribs and ran her fingers across his cheeks. "How can this be? No sé," she repeated. A timid smile crept across her face as she stepped up to the landing and circled her son. The towel slid from Amerigo's foot.

"Dios mío!" Amerigo's mother cried, pressing one hand to her mouth and wrapping the other around her jiggling apron. Though not obese, and a pageant contender in her prime, Amerigo knew his mother enjoyed sampling the culinary creations she prepared for him.

"Cosa c'è?" Amerigo's father called out. He sounded angry as he trudged through the kitchen. Amerigo felt his stomach twist in knots. He knew his father had no patience for his mother's histrionics and even less if they involved him, which was often. When his father looked up the stairs, Amerigo turned white. His father looked like he was ready to brawl. "Chi è questo?" he growled.

"It's me, Dad," Amerigo squeaked. "It's Amerigo." His foot began to throb, a sensation that felt more like a headache than something emanating from a limb.

"What kind of joke is this?" His father climbed a few stairs, ready to provoke a fight. The hair on his burly arms seemed to rise like an animal's to enlarge his stature.

At that moment Amerigo's older sister wandered out of her room. Polly yawned as she adjusted her nightgown and rubbed sleep from her eyes; she had returned from her shift at the hospital only an hour earlier. "What is going on out here?' she complained.

"It's as noisy as the ward on a full moon." When Polly focused on the scene, she stopped, and her eyes grew wide. "Amerigo?" she said, flipping her glossy black hair over her shoulder to get a better look. Polly made up for her brother's corpulence with a petite figure, both slight and firm.

Amerigo hastily explained to his assembled family how his prayers had been answered: how he'd awoken to a brand-new body. "Except for the foot," he said, flexing his petrified toes.

Polly kneeled to examine Amerigo's foot. "I don't like it," she announced after stroking, poking, and testing it for reflexes. "We should get you to the hospital."

"But I feel great!" Amerigo declared. "Mira! Maybe my foot will get better too. Especially since I'm not so fat anymore."

Polly grimaced at her brother's lame logic. "Maybe that's why you're not so fat anymore."

"What do you mean, Polly?" Amerigo's mother asked.

"I mean, maybe that's where the rest of Amerigo went."

"Sciocchezze!" Amerigo's father said. "Come here, boy." He beckoned to Amerigo to follow him down the stairs.

When Amerigo took his first step down, however, the board beneath his foot splintered. Amerigo looked sheepishly at his family's exclamations and concern.

Polly smiled and folded her arms. "Let's weigh that thing," she said.

With help from his father, Amerigo made it to the kitchen table, where his mother had prepared his usual breakfast of eggs, sausage, pancakes, toast, cereal, milk, and a wedge of melon. Amerigo salivated at the sight of the food, which he ate with abandon while his family argued what to do, and his sister tried to weigh his foot.

"Es un milagro," Amerigo's mother said. She stroked her boy's hair the way she would when he was five, and she admired the beauty of his lithe adolescent physique.

"Si," Amerigo's father agreed. But where Amerigo's mother embraced her son's overnight transformation, Amerigo's father remained suspicious. So did Polly.

"It's a miracle, all right," Polly said. "Except for the eight hundred pound gorilla—I mean foot—in the room."

When Amerigo asked for a second breakfast helping of equal proportion, and then a third, his parents murmured. Even for the nearly five hundred pound version of their son this was a lot of food.

"Pig," Polly said to her brother. "You wake up thin for the first time since you were riding a tricycle, and instead of showing some restraint, you're in an even bigger hurry to get as fat as a house."

But Amerigo just shrugged, accepting the criticism as complacently as he always had, burying his true feelings in the mountain of confections and carbohydrates his mother couldn't help but supply. As he ate, he continued to exclaim how good he felt and how he hardly felt full at all. In truth, he felt uncomfortably full, painfully full, and his foot, the disfigured one, throbbed, but how could he help himself? Eating was what he loved to do. And his mother had always made it easy, putting the food in front of him, expanding her supply to meet his ever-increasing demand. Somehow, Amerigo had always eaten it, accepting the challenge, no matter how much there was. When he was younger, he often felt disgusted after gorging. Eventually, he learned to live with his own disgust the way he imagined a caged animal learned to live with its own reek.

It was Polly, fumbling around beneath the table to try to get the scale positioned right, who soon figured out that the more Amerigo ate, the heavier his foot got. During the short course of his breakfast, it even seemed to grow, if that was possible.

Amerigo shrugged at all the concern. "It's a miracle," he said, taking up his mother's refrain. "I'm gonna enjoy it. Who knows how I'll wake up tomorrow?"

"You keep eating like that, and you won't wake up tomorrow," Polly said, shaking her head. "I always said you had one foot in the grave. Now you really do."

Amerigo's father grunted with amusement.

Although he would never admit it, Amerigo did notice after he finished his third gluttonous helping that his foot felt considerably worse, throbbing and itching between the toes.

Even though she ridiculed him as usual, Amerigo could tell by the look on Polly's face that his sister was worried, more than usual, and that worried him. Over the years, she'd been the only real advocate for his health and an endless source of strife for Amerigo and their family.

Polly phoned several doctors she knew at the hospital. After a few minutes, she'd lined up at least two specialists to see Amerigo later that morning. At first, Amerigo complained about going, but when he tried to get back up the stairs, and he realized that his foot did, in fact, seem heavier, and the pain was nearly unbearable, he reluctantly agreed.

* * *

A few hours later, Amerigo sat in a hospital bed wearing blue patient fatigues. He frowned at his sister, who sat in the visitor's chair across from him. Polly periodically erupted with laughter as she recounted for one of Amerigo's nurses their bus trip to the hospital.

"Enough!" the mild-tempered Amerigo shouted when Polly began to describe Amerigo's most humiliating moment of their journey, which occurred while waiting at the bus stop outside their apartment. A stray dog had walked up and—thinking Amerigo's foot was some new neighborhood post to which he must stake his claim—promptly watered it. Amerigo could not move his foot fast enough to escape the yellow torrent. Luckily, the toughness of its new hide repelled the urine, and his foot dried as quickly as polished marble.

Amerigo sighed with relief when the doctor walked in and interrupted Polly's story.

"So, Amerigo," the doctor said, perusing the clipboard attached to the end of the bed before even glancing at his patient. "What brings—" Catching sight of Amerigo's foot, the doctor dropped the board; it clanged against the bed frame.

After gaping at the monumental appendage for several moments, during which time Polly rose to join him, staring too, as if seeing the curiosity for the first time, the doctor said gruffly, "Is this some kind of hoax?"

Amerigo shrank into the bed. Only Polly's reputation and poignant explanation of events prevented the doctor from storming out of the room.

"OK," he sighed. "Let's do this by the book." Not trusting the numbers on the chart, the doctor ran through Amerigo's vital signs, shaking his head and concluding, finally, "The boy seems to be in perfect health."

"But my foot," Amerigo said in a small voice. Doctors made him nervous. Over the years, they never had anything good to say about his increasingly fleshy condition.

"Let's have a look at that," the doctor said as nonchalantly as if he were preparing to examine a cut that might require a few stitches. Polly hunched over the doctor so that Amerigo couldn't see what they were doing.

"My God, it's heavy," the doctor grunted when he tried to lift it.

"I told you," Polly said.

Then the doctor peppered Amerigo with questions, trying to determine if he had any symptoms prior to his transformation. Beads of perspiration lined the fuzz on Amerigo's upper lip, and thin rivulets ran down from his sideburns. "No," he said. "No indications." He didn't want to tell the doctor that he hadn't seen either foot in years, at least not without the aid of a full-length mirror, which he shunned anyway. His foot could have turned into a bowling ball or a meat loaf, and he would never have known as long as it weighed something more or less proportionate to the rest of him and got him through his day. And he didn't want to admit that, lately, he had begun to feel like food, with which he had always associated a sense of comfort and security, was turning against him. Of course, it had made him tremendously fat, but it had begun to revolt in other ways, too. Flavors seemed flatter, less aromatic; some of his favorites, like chocolate, tasted downright rancid, and almost everything he ate nowadays gave him indigestion. Lately, and for the first time on his long, soaring climb up the scales, he wondered if he had reached a tipping point, where food had finally lost its luster in the way that any commodity loses out, in the end, to the relentless twin forces of consumption and inflation. He remembered those terms from his economics class. Should he tell the doctor that lately he had been praying each night before going to bed? Would doctors know anything about prayers?

"We'll have to run some tests," the doctor announced—rather menacingly, in Amerigo's opinion. When Polly asked which tests, the doctor remained vague. "Oh, the usual," he said, heading for the door. "And we'll want to keep him a few days," he called as he exited into the hall. "For observation."

* * *

"Don't worry, hermano," Polly said. Amerigo had endured three days of testing—scans of all kinds, biopsies, blood samples, urine tests, and more. "You'll be out of here very soon."

"But the doctors won't tell me anything," Amerigo complained. "They keep coming in and whispering to each other, and then they order more tests. And this hospital food stinks."

"The doctors don't know what's wrong," Polly said. "That's why they won't tell you anything. I heard that some specialists have flown in from all over the country to examine you and your foot."

Amerigo watched his sister smile as if to suggest that he should feel grateful to draw such esteemed attention. He did not.

Polly reached into her bag and pulled out a hefty sandwich. "Mom made this. I wasn't going to give it to you because I don't think you need it. After all, your foot seems to have contracted a little over the last few days now that you're eating normal human portions. But you're right about the food here. It stinks." Polly smiled again as she handed Amerigo the sandwich.

Amerigo tore away the wrapper and ate the food greedily.

Polly shook her head. "I have to get to work," she said. "But as soon as my shift's over, I'll try to find out what I can and come by." She rose from the side of his bed and waved. "Su con la vita! Mom and Dad said they would be by later to say hi."

* * *

35

When Polly returned to his room later that day, Amerigo was no longer feeling sorry for himself. Four doctors huddled around his foot, arguing in low but strained tones. Amerigo's mother's face had assumed the blanched hue of the linens as she squeezed her son's hand and listened to the doctors with alarm. In contrast, Amerigo grinned at what he heard, and Amerigo's father watched the ball game on TV, pretending not to be bothered by the tension surrounding his son.

"Qué pasa?" Polly asked, deliberately breaking up the doctor's huddle as she made her way to her frightened mother.

"No sé," her mother whispered, leaning her head on her daughter's shoulder.

"They're cutting it off, Pol," Amerigo announced, looking pleased.

"What!" Polly looked shocked.

"That's what they're arguing about."

"But they can't do that."

Amerigo shrugged like he thought amputation was not a bad option.

"Perché?" she said to no one in particular. She flexed her fingers, forming fists and releasing them. Amerigo felt the sudden tension he always felt when Polly took a position.

Polly turned to face her father. "Dad, what do you think?"

Her father shrugged. "Not a good day for the Mets."

"Screw the Mets!" Polly shouted. "Your son's about to lose his leg!"

Grabbing hold of the nearest doctor's shoulder, Polly demanded, "I want to know what's going on!"

"Please calm down, you're upsetting the patients," the doctor said.

"I work in this hospital," Polly said, brandishing the badge pinned to her chest. "And I can tell you that nothing upsets patients and their families more than a gaggle of arrogant doctors keeping them in the dark!"

Polly's father smiled at his daughter's fiery outburst, and her mother folded her arms in approval. But Amerigo frowned. He didn't want Polly to mess up his chances of getting rid of his ball and chain. Ever since he heard the doctors' recommendations, he had begun to imagine a life in which he could eat at will and never gain weight. If it meant having a fake leg, so what. He would even settle for a wooden peg if it meant a clean slate. He was never good at sports, anyway. Besides, he saw lots of documentaries on TV about soldiers getting mechanical legs that allowed them to move around without wheelchairs. Some even ran in marathons! All he needed was something to get him up and down the stairs at home and school.

Amerigo grit his teeth. "Pol!" he said, trying to calm his sister. He reached for her hand. She shook it off, determined not to back down from the staring contest that had ensued with the closest doctor.

"Fine," the doctor sighed. "Beth," he said, pointing to one of his colleagues. "Why don't you fill them in?"

The doctor named Beth stepped forward and cleared her throat. "We've taken X-rays, MRIs, a CT scan, and numerous ultrasounds. We've biopsied several layers of the tissue. We've run every blood test we can think of."

"And?" Polly said, sounding unimpressed.

"We really don't know."

"Don't know what?"

"We don't know what the foot is made of. It's organic, we know that, but it's also machine-like. Some kind of flesh substitute. It doesn't match any living form of skin, muscle, fat, bone, tendon, cartilage—anything we've ever seen before. Man or beast."

"How did it get there?"

"We don't know."

"What happened to the rest of my brother?" Polly pressed.

"We don't know. But it seems to have settled in his foot."

"And that's all you've figured out?" Polly said, flapping her hands in the air.

The doctor looked equally exasperated. "What did you want us to figure out?"

"Is it life threatening?"

"It doesn't seem to be. He's healthy in all other respects. Very healthy. In fact, none of his prior ailments—high blood pressure, diabetes, atherosclerosis, apnea, you know, the usual symptoms of obesity—none of those have persisted."

"Then why do you want to cut it off?"

"Well, there are several good reasons," the doctor said. She looked down her nose at Polly. "For one thing, it appears to be immobilizing—"

"Yeah," Amerigo interrupted, agreeing more enthusiastically than he intended. "It's immobilizing."

"Well, why don't we see if disciplined diet and exercise will help reduce its size? I mean, my brother's been fat since he could recite the alphabet. Maybe this is a wakeup call. Maybe, just maybe, if this happened to my brother it will happen to others as well. Maybe it's the start of some new epidemic. God only knows what new chemicals the food industry's throwing at us."

The doctors murmured and raised their eyebrows.

Polly pressed her point. "Will you go around amputating everyone's limbs? It's medieval!"

"Stop it!" Amerigo shouted at his sister. "It's my foot. I want them to cut it off." It sounded strange to hear himself so readily abandon something that had grown with him and supported him all his life just so that he could look good and, more importantly, go on consuming without paying the usual price. After spending so many days and nights alone in the hospital, Amerigo had reflected on his life and state of affairs. In the dark, lonely hours on his ward, he'd convinced himself that God had answered his prayers and presented him with a great gift. But Amerigo knew enough of his faith to know that divine intervention always came with a price. Just as the prophets of the Bible had to make great sacrifices to receive and deliver their epiphanies, so Amerigo would have to sacrifice too. Luckily, it was just a foot God was demanding in exchange for a life of infinite calories. That was his theory. Amerigo had not had the courage to confirm it with the doctors, or with anyone else for that matter.

Beth, the doctor, looked scornfully at Polly. "We could try putting him on a restricted diet," she suggested. "But it's possible that this stony tissue," she smacked Amerigo's foot with a latex-gloved hand, "has a viral nature. If it extends to his vital organs—well, it's unlikely he would survive."

"Are you saying it's a form of cancer?" Polly asked, maintaining her look of defiance.

"I'm only saying, what if?" the doctor replied, turning back to her colleagues.

"Amerigo," Polly turned to her brother. "Why would you want such a thing?"

"Because Pol, you don't know what it's like to be me. I feel like...I feel like it's a miracle." How could he explain that he had long ago given up ever imagining himself thin, as if such self-regard belonged to other boys and other people but not to him? How could he confess that his obesity had become such a curse that he sometimes wanted to die? He had no real friends anymore, mostly because his extreme corpulence and all of its accompanying indignities embarrassed people. Plus, he never had the energy to do much more than what a skeletal routine allowed. How could he make others see what he saw so clearly: that he would have to sacrifice something to be worthy of this divine gift? How could he suggest that a foot was nothing compared to the new life he had just begun to taste? But even as he clung to such justification, its fallibility nagged at him. Something the doctor had said. *Machine-like.* The phrase struck a nerve. Was he taking the easy way out? A tear escaped, but he quickly brushed it away.

"You...you've always been perfect, Pol," Amerigo said bitterly. "How could you understand?"

Polly stared at her brother, who stared back, refusing to back down as he ordinarily would. Polly sighed. She looked at her mother and father, who seemed bewildered, each in their own way.

"Fine," she said. "But you're making a terrible mistake. And for what, Amerigo? You can't consume your way to happiness. There are no elixirs, even if these doctors try to convince you there are. You might feel better for a little while, but you'll be worse off for taking their shortcut."

Something Polly said rattled one of the doctors. Or maybe that doctor had been arguing against the other three. "For the record," he said, stepping away from his colleagues, "I would not recommend surgery at this time. I am calling for a strict dietary regimen supplemented by extreme doses of statin."

"Statin?" Amerigo and his family said with one voice.

"Yes. The predominant organic compound in the biopsies appears to be lipid-based. Thus, it is my feeling that we may be able to break down the deposits by attacking them with a cholesterol-lowering drug. You're very lucky, young man, that this tissue settled in your foot and not in your arteries!"

"You're all nuts!" Polly shouted and stormed out of the room.

* * *

Amerigo sat at the kitchen table, alone. He could hear his mother humming to herself as she moved through her daily chores. Polly and his father were at work. It had been more than a month since the amputation and, until recently, everything seemed to be going according to Amerigo's plan. He was getting used to his artificial foot, which enabled him to maneuver much more adeptly than the five-hundred-pound skin suit he used to wear. And, even better, he'd been able to eat with abandon without growing fatter. Polly said that she refused to watch him kill himself, so she boycotted family meals. Amerigo's mother seemed to be as happy as ever to have her son's handsome features back. Preparing all of that food for him every day did not seem to bother her. Amerigo's father still treated him with indifference, largely ignoring the changed condition of his son. Without saying so, he seemed to side with Polly.

Amerigo stared at the buffet his mother had prepared for his lunch. It covered every inch of the table. On any other day, he would have been halfway through this feast. Not today. Today, his prime pursuit had taken on a sinister manner. Where once his trusty pastry and delicatessen subjects served his voraciousness, today they looked hostile and unfamiliar. Even the fruit, which Amerigo had always considered the most innocent confection, had taken on an evil hue. He reached under the table to touch his remaining foot, which throbbed and ached at the sight of so many calories amassed like enemy troops; it ached enough to shake him to his foundation.

Two days ago, Amerigo's idyllic new world fractured like a shell when his good foot mysteriously started to itch. He thought its skin had begun to look shinier, maybe a little metallic, its texture stony. It frightened him. He wore long pants and tube socks to hide the budding transformation. Last night, his foot had begun to throb, and this morning it would not fit into his shoe. Not even close.

Amerigo shoved the heaping plates and bowls away. They rattled like gunfire as they struck the linoleum and shattered in rapid succession. He pounded his fists on the empty table and glared angrily at the steaming piles and oozing puddles on the floor. His lips trembled.

"Amerigo?" his mother called.

Amerigo hid his face in his hands. He hated his mother for providing so willingly. He hated his father for having nothing to say. He hated his sister for being so perfect. But mostly, he hated himself. He had buried himself under a mountain of calories, feeding his flesh, starving his soul. Along the way, he stopped caring about the consequences, and he stopped thinking about his future, pushing them out of his mind as if they were someone else's problem. He hated himself for giving up so easily, not just his foot—that was but a symbol of what he'd relinquished day after day, year after year.

Was it too late to save himself?

Amerigo shuddered.

Even if he could save himself, what would he be saving? He looked down from his mechanical foot to the one that had begun to transform. *Dio mio,* he mouthed. For the first time, he saw himself for what he had become: a machine, programmed to serve his own impulses, a slave to his insatiable voracity. With that dark realization, a howl of despair gathered deep in Amerigo's core and rose with volcanic intensity. The sound that erupted from his mouth was otherworldly. Nothing human about it. After that, the transformation was rapid, starting with his remaining foot and accelerating upward.

Gourgey

The last thing Amerigo heard was his mother calling his name. At that same instant, a tear froze in place on Amerigo's cheek—a tear for his forsaken foot.

To learn about the author, Bill Gourgey, please visit www.billgourgey.com.

www.ingramcontent.com/pod-product-compliance
Lightning Source LLC
Chambersburg PA
CBHW050914120626
46552CB00004B/1566